The Gaskitts ...

Oh, no!

Oh, dear!

Oh, my!

... again!

First published 2005 by Walker Books Ltd
87 Vauxhall Walk, London SE11 5HJ

This edition published 2018

2 4 6 8 10 9 7 5 3 1

Text © 2005 Allan Ahlberg
Illustrations © 2005 Katharine McEwen

The right of Allan Ahlberg and Katharine McEwen to be identified
as author and illustrator respectively of this work has been asserted by them
in accordance with the Copyright, Designs and Patents Act 1988

This book has been typeset in Stempel Schneidler,
Cafeteria, Tapioca and Kosmik

Printed in China

British Library Cataloguing in Publication Data:
a catalogue record for this book
is available from the British Library

ISBN 978-1-4063-8167-2

www.walker.co.uk

Allan Ahlberg

The Children Who Smelled a Rat

illustrated by

KATHARINE McEWEN

WALKER
BOOKS

Contents

Meet The Gaskitts

Mr Gaskitt
The dad.

Mrs Gaskitt
The mum
and taxi-driver.

Gary Gaskitt
The baby.
Eyes blue,
hair brown,
weight
~~7lb 12oz~~
~~8lb 4oz~~
9lb 10oz.

he's growing all the time

Horace Gaskitt: The cat.
Horace has lots of friends.

Mostly cats!

But not all!

Gus and Gloria Gaskitt
The twins.

He's my evil twin!

No, she's mine!

Picture dictionary
(some useful words and phrases)

| parcel | spade | seal | Crunchy Mice | jelly and ice-cream* | dungeon | flabbergasted |

*Actually, there's no jelly and ice-cream in this story, but we thought you'd like to see it, all the same.

Chapter 1
The Parcel

One winter's day a forgetful man in a green hat and a great hurry left his umbrella on a train, his briefcase in a bookshop, his book – which he had only just bought – on a park bench, and his very important parcel in a taxi.

Later on, much later actually, when the man came home again, he left his hat on his head, forgot his supper, and went to bed.*

---

* Which is the last we'll hear of him!

Meanwhile, on that same day, it was a Friday,

Mrs Gaskitt *found* a parcel in her taxi.

And when she picked it up,

the parcel went …

Chapter 2

Bye Bye, Baby

Mr Gaskitt was minding the baby.

It was his turn.

And doing the shopping

and opening the boot

and feeling in his pocket

for the car-park ticket

and tying his shoelace

and whistling a little tune

and *looking the other way.*

Meanwhile, little Gary: eyes blue,

hair brown,

weight 10lb 3oz,

was ...

Oh, no!

Oh, dear!

Oh, my!

... rolling away.

Chapter 2 ½: "Tweet, Tweet!"

Horace was at home watching the goldfish

when Mrs Gaskitt came in with the parcel,

unwrapped it, scratched her head,

had a cup of tea

and went out again.

Horace watched the parcel, and the unwrapping.

It was, of course – you guessed, didn't you? –

a little bird in a cage.

A teeny, tiny, little bird

lost and all alone …

with a cat.

Chapter 2 ³/₄: 10lb 5oz

Meanwhile, little Gary …

was still rolling away.

Oh, my!

Chapter 3
The Teacher
Who Wasn't Herself

So there we are,

a bad day for a little bird,

a bad day for a little baby,

and a bad day, too,

come to think of it,

for Gus and Gloria.

Actually, they had had a bad *week*.

On Monday

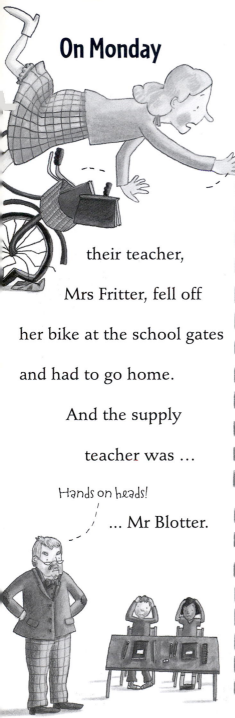

their teacher,

Mrs Fritter, fell off

her bike at the school gates

and had to go home.

And the supply

teacher was …

Hands on heads!

… Mr Blotter.

On Tuesday

Mrs Fritter came back,

tripped over a skipping ro

and went away again.

ACCIDENT BOOK

MON Mrs. Fritter
THE Mrs. Fritter
WED Mrs. Fritter

ACCIDENT B

fell off bike
sprained an
cuts + bruise

And the supply

teacher was …

Ooer! … Mr Cruncher.

On Wednesday and Thursday

Mrs Fritter was run over by a lady with a pushchair and trodden on in the doctor's waiting room.

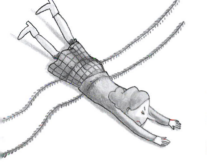

And the supply teacher was …

Alas, alack!

… Mrs Doom.

Now it was Friday, and Mrs Fritter,

with her arm in a sling, was back again,

well, sort of.

But the children were puzzled.

Mrs Fritter had a funny look in her eye.

She seemed to have forgotten

where things were kept,

and – worse still –

Where's the chalk,
Thingy?

ALL THEIR NAMES.

Chapter 4
Little Lost Bird

Horace was back at the house watching the bird.

"A bird," he thought. "A teeny,

tiny, little bird, lost and all alone."

And he thought,

"Cats eat birds ... hm."

The bird was watching

Horace. She fluffed her

feathers, flicked her

tail, opened her teeny,

tiny beak and spoke.

"Come here," said the bird.

"Er ... right," said Horace.

"Look into my eyes," said the bird.

"Right," said Horace.

"Do as I say," said the bird.

"Why should I?" said Horace.

"Do as I say!"

"Er ... right," said Horace.

Meanwhile, one teeny, tiny baby,

getting bigger though, 10lb 6oz,

was – do you remember? –

still rolling away.

Still in the shopping trolley,

but now on the back of a

lorry – did you see that? –

and being chased

by his dad.

Mr Gaskitt was

running

hard.

SKIP-IT

Actually, if he'd only known it,

he could have caught a taxi.

Mrs Gaskitt, at that very moment,

was driving by.

But Mrs Gaskitt never saw

him, or the baby.
She was watching the car in
front, sucking a humbug,
thinking of getting her
hair cut, puzzling
over that little bird,
and *looking the
other way.*

Meanwhile, back at the house ...

... said the bird.

Chapter 5

Frightening Mrs Fritter

Gus and Gloria's class liked Mrs Fritter.

She was the kindest,

SILENCE, THINGY!

friendliest,

THINGIES – SIT STILL!

and most popular

STOP THAT, THINGY!

teacher in the whole school.

Well, usually.

But today, as you can see and *hear* –

LOST YOUR BOOK? MONSTROUS!

things (and thingies) were different.

Mrs Fritter frightened

everybody.

She frightened Randolph,

the class rat, who hid in his cage,

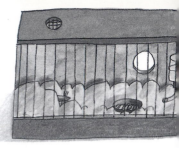

and Mr Blagg,

the headmaster,

who hid in his office.

When Mr Cruncher

came back

for his dumbbells,

she even frightened him.

The children whispered

and passed little notes

to each other,

and smelled a rat.

Actually, they really did smell a rat.

Mrs Fritter wouldn't let them

clean Randolph's cage out.

They smelled a couple of

gerbils too, and a hamster.

At playtime

Mrs Fritter went to the staffroom

and ...

MORE TEA,
MR THINGY?

frightened the teachers.

Mr Blagg sneaked in, grabbed a cup of coffee

and a Kit Kat and sneaked out again.

Back in the classroom Randolph

sneaked out for a bit of biscuit.

Out in the playground

Gus, Gloria and the others

frowned and scratched their heads,

cudgelled their little brains

and ran around ...

... and *shouted*.

"What's going on?"

"Stop shovin' ... Thingy!"

"It's a puzzle to me!"

"And me!"

"And me!"

"Shoot, shoot!"

"I think –"*

"My name's not 'Thingy'!"

"It's a mystery to me!"

"She's a changed woman!"

Meanwhile, Mrs Fritter stood

staring out of the staffroom window.

Spots of rain had begun to fall.

Mrs Fritter ... yes.

She was a changed woman, all right:

Longer Hair

(A)

A perfectly good
arm in a sling

Different perfume

(B)

Non-existent
cuts and bruises

The rain was streaking the glass.

The face behind it seemed to waver

and dissolve,

and *shift its shape.*

Ooer!

Chapter 6
Look into My Eyes

Back at the house –

no bird seed to be found –

the bird was pecking

grumpily at a little bowl

of Crunchy Mice.

"They make Crunchy Canaries as well,"

said Horace.

"No, they don't," said the bird.

Later on the bird began

to complain about her cage.

"It's rubbish, this cage," she tweeted.

"Too small – too draughty,

and it needs a good clean."

Horace, meanwhile, had crouched down

on his tummy,

and was creeping out of the room.

"Come here," said the bird.

And she said, "Open this cage."

"No!" said Horace.

"You'll escape!

You'll get lost!

I'll get into trouble!

I'll..."

"Look into my eyes," said the bird.

So, anyway,

the bird sat in the window looking out

at the traffic, while Horace cleaned the cage.

"Put clean newspaper on the floor," said the bird.

"Fill the water bottle. Polish the mirror."

Horace had mixed feelings.

He disliked being bossed about

by a little bundle of feathers.

On the other hand (or paw),

the truth is, he admired the bird.

(And the goldfish,

by the way,

admired him.)

"This bird is cleverer than Randolph,"

thought Horace.

(Horace had met Randolph in an earlier story.)*

And he thought, "I could learn a thing or two."

The bird, meanwhile,

was gazing back into the room.

She fluttered down, perched on Horace's head

and tweeted in his ear. Phone for a pizza!

* *The Cat Who Got Carried Away*: Walker Books, £5.99
"Grand and gripping." *The Daily Vet*
"Worth every penny!" Allan Ahlberg

Chapter 7

Up and Away

Oh, no!

Meanwhile, little Gary Gaskitt

– remember him? –

was *still* rolling away.

Well, up and away really.

Look what's happened

since we saw him last.

SKIP-IT

This is ridiculous, isn't it?

Whoever saw such a thing?

As fast as Gary is gaining weight

– 10lb 8oz now! –

his poor old father

is losing it.

Puff, puff!

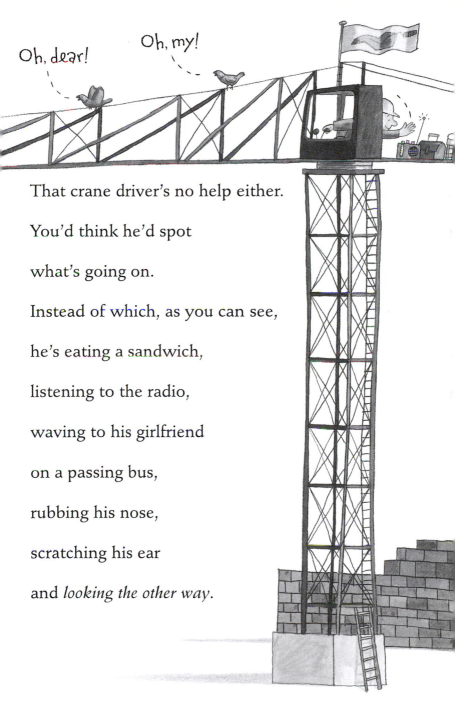

Oh, dear!

Oh, my!

That crane driver's no help either.

You'd think he'd spot

what's going on.

Instead of which, as you can see,

he's eating a sandwich,

listening to the radio,

waving to his girlfriend

on a passing bus,

rubbing his nose,

scratching his ear

and *looking the other way*.

Chapter 8

Beethoven and Spinach

Back in the classroom

things were going from bad to worse.

Mrs Fritter lost her temper

over the slightest thing:

a speck of dust	MONSTROUS!
a dropped pin	SILENCE!
even ... breathing.	THINGY!

Her comments were contradictory,

or sometimes just plain crazy.

Gus, Gloria and the others

could not tell

if they were coming or going.

In the afternoon for their music lesson

all they heard was Bach, Beethoven and Brahms.

And in home economics

all they cooked was spinach pie.

At the end of the day

Mr Blagg poked his head

round the classroom door,

flinched and disappeared again.

Randolph stayed out of sight altogether.

He smelled a rat too.

Till, at last – Yippee! – home-time.

Mrs Fritter, with a huge umbrella

in her hand and a wild look in her eye,

charged out of the classroom,

across the playground,

through the

school gates ...

... and away.

I can't phone for a pizza –
I'm a cat!

Yes, you can.

No, I can't!

Yes, you can.

No, I can't!

Look into
my eyes ...

Yes, I can.

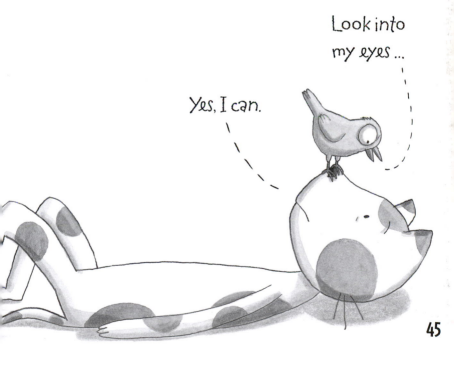

Chapter 9

The Face

It was a wet and gloomy afternoon.

Street lights were beginning to shine.

Cars had their headlights on.

A little gang of boys and girls came dodging

and weaving along, in and out of shop doorways,

hiding behind wide ladies and phone boxes,

on the trail of a huge umbrella.

There was Gus and Gloria, of course (it's *their* book),

Molly and Tracey and Tom,

Rupert, Eric and Esmeralda.

Mrs Fritter marched down the High Street

in a straight line.

Large men and fierce-looking dogs

leapt out of her way.

Sensitive infants caught sight

of her wild gaze and burst into tears.

Gus, Gloria and the others stuck to the trail.

A left turn here. A right turn there.

A gate – a gravel path – a house.

The house was tall and dark.

Mrs Fritter climbed the front steps;

switched on the porch light.

The children in the shrubbery

crouched and watched.

They saw her open the door and step inside.

They saw her in the doorway

looking back into the street.

And they saw,

they really did,

at the very same time,

her *face,* all watery

and wavering

behind the glass –

one floor below! –

at the basement

window.

Phew!

Chapter 10

In the Dungeon

Yes, phew!

Mrs Fritter's body

in the doorway.

Mrs Fritter's face at the window.

The children were astounded, astonished,

and – what's the word? – *flabbergasted*.

Well, no sooner had the front door

closed on Mrs Fritter No.1, than down

the basement steps they scrambled

to peer in through the barred

and dusty window at Mrs Fritter No.2.

She was sitting on the floor with a broken chair

beside her and a hopeful look in her eye.

The door was locked,

but Gloria found a key under the mat.

Once inside, the children took one look:

broken chair, fallen teacher –

sniffed one sniff: familiar perfume –

and guessed it all.

Of course, this was

the *real* Mrs Fritter.

The other one,

the mad imposter,

was...

8:30 A.M.

No marmalade?
MONSTROUS!

"My *sister*, boys and girls, here on a visit."

Mrs Fritter brushed a cobweb from her hair.

"Gets funny turns sometimes."

"Not that funny, Miss!"

"Anyway, she was a bit upset this morning, and sort of tied me up and locked me in down here. I've only just got loose."

Well, the children were astounded

all over again,

astonished,

and – what's the word? – *affronted.*

"She's not your sister, Miss!" they cried.

"That's right!"

"No way!"

"She's your …

EVIL TWIN!*

*Which was actually what Gus had been trying to say back there (p31) in the playground. Fancy that!

Then,

just when things were going well,

and the rain had stopped,

and the sky was clear,

and a little bird (no, not that one)

was singing sweetly in the garden,

and the children were congratulating

themselves on a puzzle,

a *conundrum* solved ...

a shadowy figure

came down the basement steps

and slammed the door –

and locked it.

Chapter 11

Elsewhere ...

this was happening:

1. Horace

Horace had sneaked out of the room

while the bird was looking the other way.

He was halfway

    to his friend's house,

        taking a short cut

           through somebody's garden

        and, at that very moment,

only two doors away from

    Mrs Fritter's house. Hm.

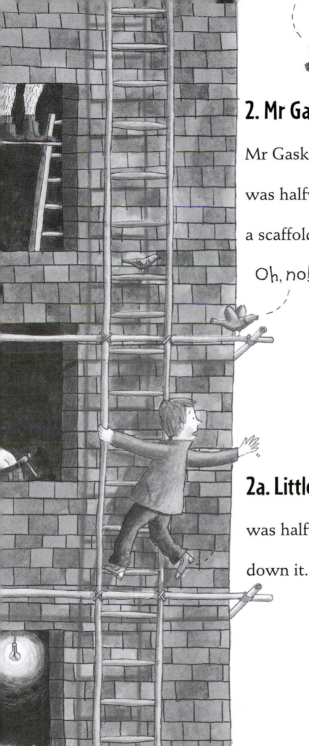

2. Mr Gaskitt (11st 9lb)

Mr Gaskitt – Puff, puff! –

was halfway up

a scaffold, while

Oh, no!

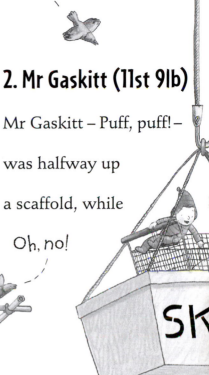

SK

2a. Little Gary

was halfway

down it.

3. The Bird

The bird was taking a bath

and singing sweetly.

She loves you,
tweet, tweet, tweet!

Horace, under orders, had found the bath

and a few other things

in Gus and Gloria's toy cupboard.

The pizza was, for now, forgotten.

4. Mrs Gaskitt

Mrs Gaskitt –

not seen much of her lately,

have we? –

was rather busy,

also at that very moment,

with a tattooed lady and a man in a gorilla suit.

More later.

Chapter 12

Digging Like Mad!

Back in the basement the situation was ... *Tricky!*

The doors were locked, the windows barred.

The children's mobile phones were lost,

or left at home, or not charged up.

Their shouts – screams, even –

would never be heard on the faraway street.

And Mrs Fritter's evil twin

was out in the garden ... with a spade.

"Fond of gardening, she is," said Mrs Fritter.

But Gloria (on the table) saw things differently.

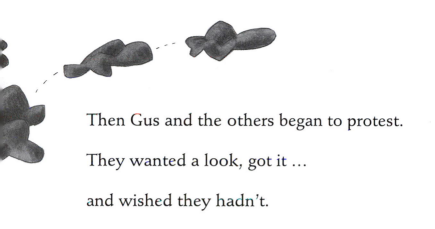

Then Gus and the others began to protest.

They wanted a look, got it …

and wished they hadn't.

A hole!

Oh, no!

A trench!

Oh, dear!

A pit!

Oh, my!

A grave?

Ooer

Chapter 12a: **Horace the Hero**

Now the basement door was heavy and thick

with great big hinges,

a massive lock ... and a cat flap.

A cat flap. Hm.

Too small to escape through, of course.

Unless, that is, you were a...

Horace, at that very moment,

was making his way

along the garden wall to his friend's house.

And Horace was a cat, wasn't he?

He could do it.

Yes! Yippee! Hooray!

In through the cat flap.

Take a message in his collar.

(If he had a collar.)

Yes, Horace to

the rescue!

Horace the Hero!

He would love it,

wouldn't he?

Only trouble was,

Horace never saw the faces at the window,

or heard the faint shouts from the house.

He was watching his step

on the slippery wall

(and that scary woman with the spade),

puzzling over the bossy bird,

thinking of all the things

he would tell his friend,

and *looking the other way.*

67

Chapter 12b: Tricky Situation No.2

As for little Gary, that teeny, tiny baby, that brave little bundle – look what's happening to him now.

He's up the creek and down the river. All at sea!

Who'd believe it?

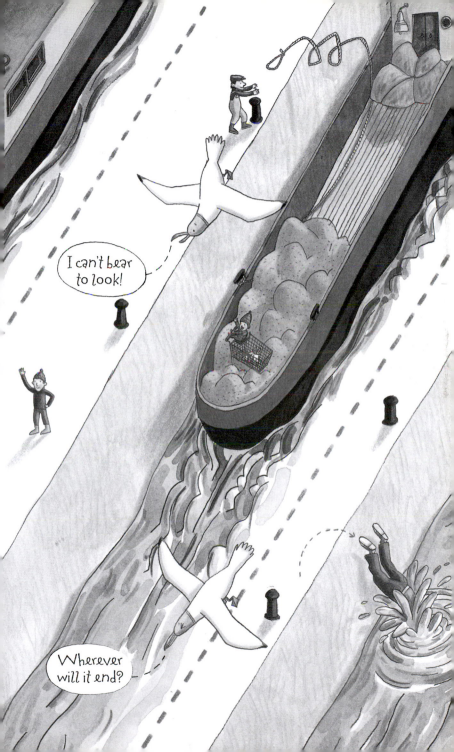

Chapters 13, 14 and 15

The Simplified Version

Look into my eyes!

Meanwhile – Oh dear, tricky situation No.3 – we're running out of space. Only a few pages left and loads of words still to write. We'll have to squashtheminabit.

Or make 'em smaller. Can you read this at the back? This is too small, isn't it? And this is absolutely ridiculous. How about this? Better? Are you sure? Right – off we go. So here we are. Back in the basement, Gus, Gloria and the others were scratching their heads and puzzling over how to escape. Out in the garden Mrs Fritter's evil twin had almost disappeared. The hole was deep and getting deeper. The sky was dark and getting darker. Rain was falling again ... and Horace had given up on visiting his friend and was hurrying home. The bird, meanwhile, was fooling around in her little cage, with a mirror, and feeling lonely. Tweet, tweet! Meanwhile also, Mrs Gaskitt was having a tricky situation of her own with a man on stilts and a seal. Something to do with a circus. But that's another story. We'll have to skip it. This is the simplified version.*

Smash the door down!

Dig a tunnel!

Anyway – Puff, puff! – let's keep moving. There's thunder and lightning now. Mrs Fritter No.2 is banging around in the tool shed. What's she up to? What's going on? Look out, here she comes! Meanwhile, Horace is climbing in through his own cat flap, the little bird is reading the paper, and Mr Gaskitt is ... swimming? Well Mrs Fritter No.2 is almost swimming.

*Mrs Gaskitt does have her own story, though, in case you're interested:
The Woman Who Won Things: Walker Books, £5.99
"Unputdownable!" Allan Ahlberg's mother
"Worth a knighthood." The Queen

There's a torrent of rain out there ... and – yes, here she comes – lit up in the lightning flashes – closer and closer – down the steps – the children can see her! – with a key in one hand – Mrs Gaskitt's taxi, by the way, has broken down and a great big hairy man is fixing it. Where were we? Yes, a key in one hand – CRASH! BANG! (lightning) – and – Oh, no! Oh, dear! Oh, my! – an axe in the other.

An axe. **An AXE**? Oops. Sorry about that.

"She looks a bit upset to me," said Mrs Fritter.

The children, Gus and Gloria, Molly and Tracey and Tom, Rupert, Eric and Esmeralda, agreed.

"She's got an axe, Miss!" they cried.

"She's got a *key*."

"Oh, mother..."

"She'll catch her death of cold out there," said Mrs Fritter. And now, the key is in the lock! The door is swinging open! 'The End' is near! Too near, actually. No room for pictures now – no space at all. *Not even for a teeny, tiny frog?* No, hoppit.

Where were we? The End – yes. There she stands in the doorway, Mrs Fritter's evil twin, with a mad look in her eyes and an axe in her hand. Whereupon – who'd believe it? – another lady comes marching down the steps, opens her mouth and,

"MARIGOLD, COME HERE!
PUT DOWN THAT AXE!
DON'T ARGUE!
LOOK INTO MY EYES!"

The children were amazed, of course, flabbergasted, it goes without saying, and delighted. Mrs Fritter seemed pleased too. "Chloe!" she cried. "What a pleasant surprise." And then the penny dropped. Oh, dear –

no room to swing a cat even. **MIAOW?**

We'll really have to squeeze this in. Sorry. Anyway, yes, the children took one look at this *familiar* lady No.3 ...

… and guessed it all.

TRIP

LETS!

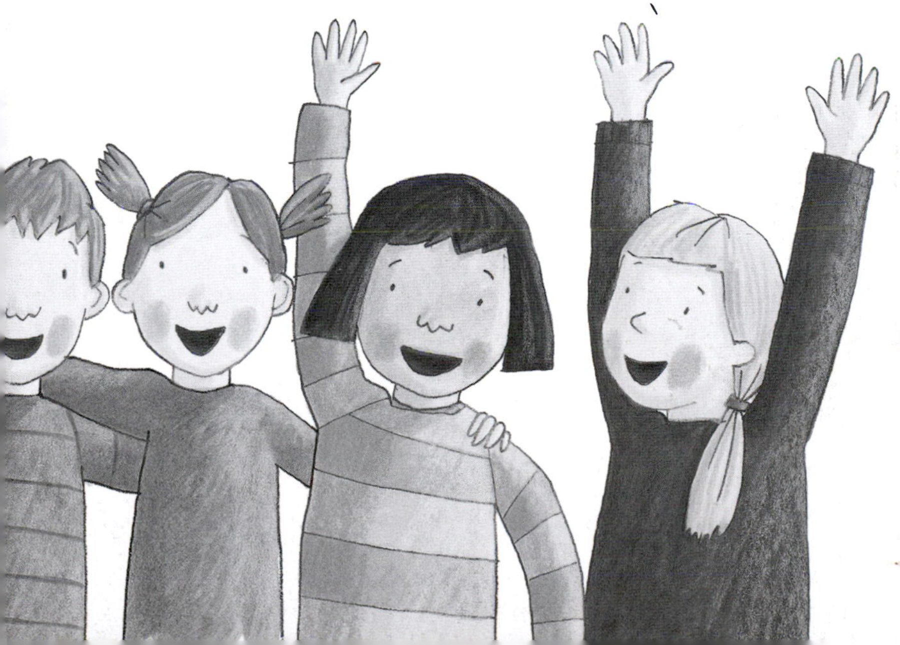

Chapter 16

Happy Endings

1. The Bird and Horace

When Horace came home and found that teeny,

tiny bird (lost and all alone) *reading the paper*,

he admired her even more.

"Wish I was clever," he said.

"Wish I could read."

"No problemo," said the bird.

She fluttered up and perched on Horace's head.

"I'll teach you."

c-a-t Yippee!

I can read!

Now I'm gonna learn ... French!

2. Mr Gaskitt and The Baby

Meanwhile, in a cafe

down by the docks,

little Gary Gaskitt: hair damp, eyes shut,

weight 10lb 3½oz,*

was safe and sound.

So was the shopping.

Mr Gaskitt was safe

and sound too, and

soaking wet,

of course.

And sleepy.

Sweet dreams,

Mr Gaskitt!

*Yes, 4½ oz lighter, minus one nappy – Poo!

3. Mrs Fritter and The Children

Back in the basement

Mrs Fritter No.2 had apologized

to Mrs Fritter No.1.

Mrs Fritter No.3 had given

Mrs Fritter No.1 a powerful hug

and taken Mrs Fritter No.2

home in her car.

Of course, their names

weren't *all* Mrs Fritter.

That would be silly, wouldn't it?

No, No.2 was Mrs Trotter

and No.3 was Mrs Molotovski.

So that sorts that out.

Meanwhile *now*, Mrs Fritter

– minus her alarming sisters –

is upstairs in the kitchen with Gus and Gloria,

Molly and Tracey and Tom,

Rupert, Eric and Esmeralda

eating *jelly and ice-cream*.

There wasn't supposed to *be* any jelly and

ice-cream – remember? – but never mind.

This *is* the happy ending after all.

Oh, yes, and finally…

4. Mrs Gaskitt and...

Meanwhile also,

Mrs Gaskitt had said goodbye to the circus

and was back in her taxi.

When she arrived home

she found a *parcel* on the back seat.

And when she picked it up,

Oh, no!

Oh, dear!

Oh, my!

the parcel went ...

Oink! *

*Fancy that.